A Scarf and a Half

by Amanda Brandon

Illustrated by Catalina Echeverri

Granny Mutton loved to knit.

CLICKETY CLICK...

flicked her needles, all day long.

She knitted **cosy shawls** for **baby lambs** and...

Woolly hats for chilly rams' horns...

and **snuggly socks** for shivering sheep-dogs.

One day she made a
dazzling rainbow scarf
for Little Lionel's
birthday and
it grew...
and grew...
and grew.

"Stop Granny, stop!"
her friends said.

"That's not a scarf,
that's a scarf and a half!"

So Granny Mutton cast off
her final stitch.

She smoothed and rolled
and wrapped the scarf,
then she tied it with a bow
and gave it to Little Lionel
with her love.

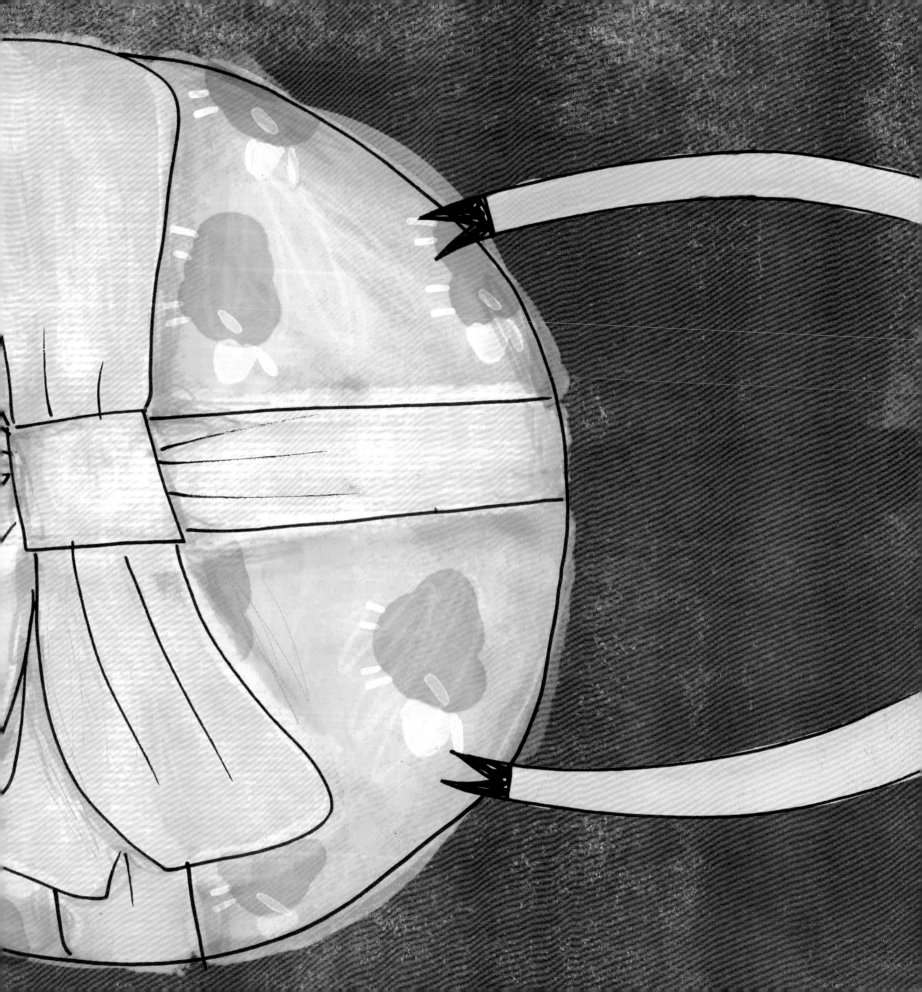

Little Lionel was **excited**. He was sure
that Granny's present was a **football**.

He couldn't wait to play. He **ripped** open the paper but...

...it was a **flippy**, **floppy** scarf.

"You can't have a laugh with a scarf,"
he said crossly.

But Granny Mutton couldn't hear
because his voice was muffled in wool.

Little Lionel went out
in his scarf but...

It was so long he tripped and
landed in a muddy puddle.

SPLAT!

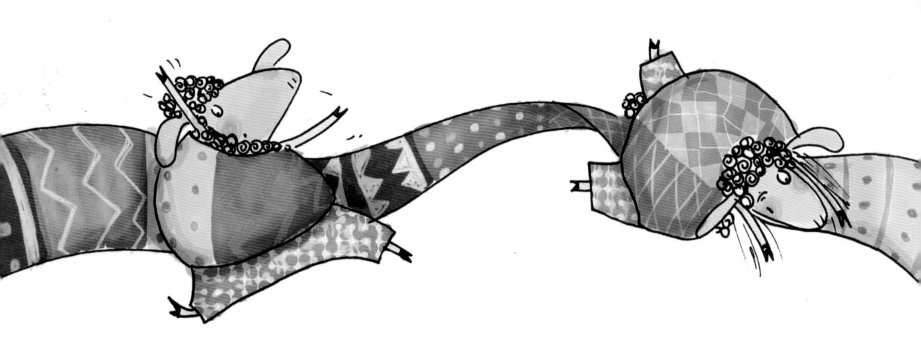

He tried **skipping** with the scarf but ...
his feet got **tangled** and he **toppled** over.

"It's no use, you can't have a laugh with a scarf," he said with a scowl and he tossed his present away.

His friend Bleater saw him looking sad.
He said, "That's not a scarf,
that's a scarf and a half!"

He **grabbed** the two ends
and tied them to the branch
of the big farmyard tree.

The two of them swung HIGH and LOW until they were dizzy.

Rocky the sheep-dog came roaring past. He took
one look and said, "That's not a scarf,
that's a scarf and a half!"

VROOM ZOOM

He tied it to his cart and said,
"Hop in. I'll take you for a ride."

Back and forth he dragged the
giggling pair until they
tumbled out.

ROCKY

Little Lionel started to cheer up and more friends came to see his **amazing** present.

"That's not a scarf,
that's a scarf and a half!"
they said and they

HAULED and PULLED

this way and that in a crazy tug of war.

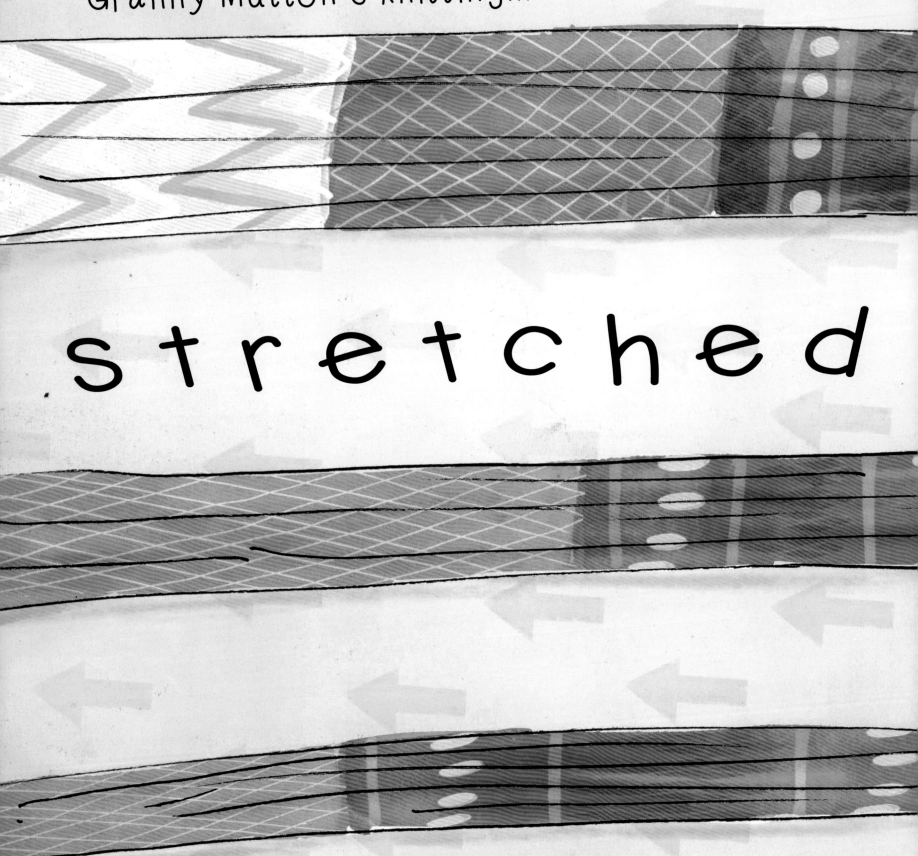

Granny Mutton's knitting...

stretched

and **strained** until...

It reached twice as long.

PING!

The laughing friends let go and landed in a HIGGLEDY PIGGLEDY pile.

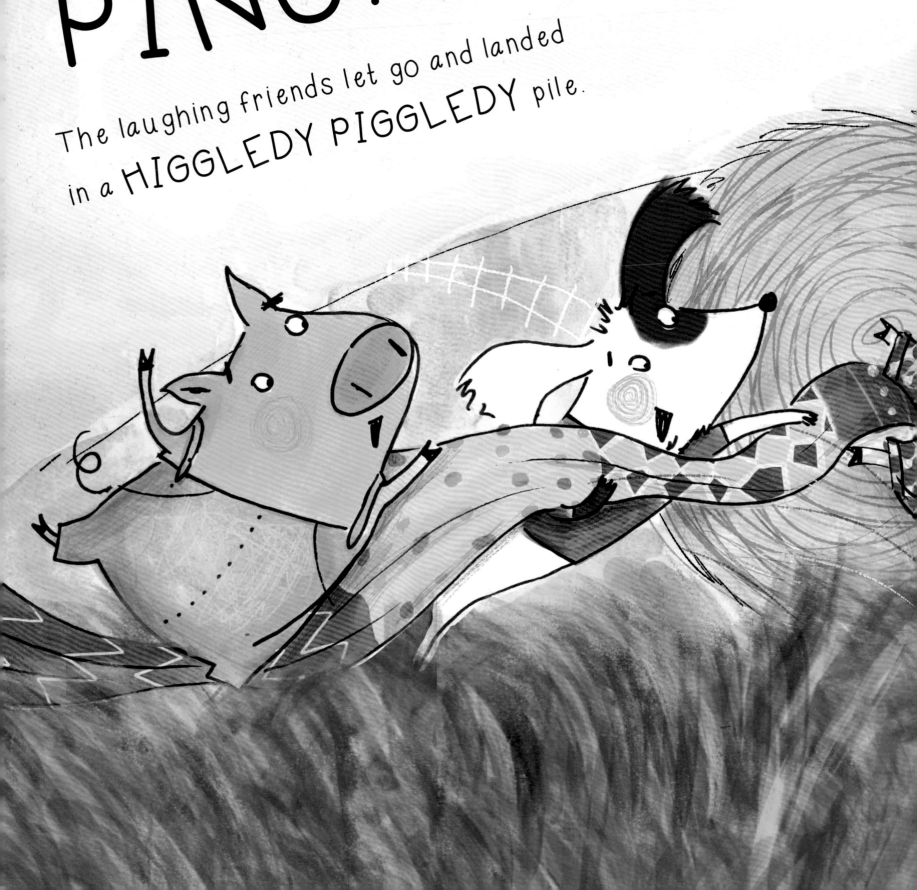

Tired but happy the friends snuggled down at Granny Mutton's house. "Not only have I got a scarf and a half," Lionel said, "I have a Granny and a half too!"

The End

A Scarf and a Half
is an original concept by © Amanda Brandon

Author: Amanda Brandon

Illustrator: Catalina Echeverri
Catalina is represented by Plum Pudding
www.plumpuddingillustration.com

Published by MAVERICK ARTS PUBLISHING LTD
Studio 3A, City Business Centre, 6 Brighton Road,
Horsham, West Sussex, RH13 5BB, +44 (0)1403 256941
© Maverick Arts Publishing Limited September 2014

A CIP catalogue record for this book is available at the British Library.

ISBN 978-1-84886-116-9

Maverick
arts publishing
www.maverickbooks.co.uk